Jo Simmons

SCHOLASTIC

First published in the UK in 2015 by Scholastic Children's Books
An imprint of Scholastic Ltd
Euston House, 24 Eversholt Street,
London, NW1 1DB, UK
Registered office: Westfield Road, Southam, Warwickshire, CV47 0RA

ISBN 978 1407 15230 1

A CIP catalogue record for this book is available from the British Library.

Printed and bound by CPI Group (UK) Ltd, Croydon, CR0 4YY
Papers used by Scholastic Children's Books are made from wood grown in
sustainable forests.

1 3 5 7 9 10 8 6 4 2

www.scholastic.co.uk

FOR SALI AND MARTHA, GYDA LLAWER O GARIAD

Chapter 1

A BIG SHOUT-OUT

It was an ordinary day. An ordinary day called Monday. Sam Lowe was on his way to school, a short walk through the streets of his home town of Topside. His friend Nina Fox, who lived on the next road, was walking with him. These two were unlikely chums. Nina was quiet and very keen on knitting. Sam, on the other hand, was loud. *Really* loud.

Already this morning, Sam's mum had told him to "Shush!" when he asked for the marmalade and then, uh-oh, Sam started humming as his mum fried some eggs. The sound was so massive it made her jump in shock, pinging a fried egg up on to the ceiling, where it stuck like an eggy flying saucer.

"For goodness' sake, Sam!" she snapped. "Can you keep your voice down?"

The answer was no. Sam couldn't keep his voice down. It wasn't his fault, though. Some children are just blessed with loud voices from the get-go. Sam was one of them. People – his mum, teachers, random strangers – were always telling Sam to SHUSH! But that was like asking a baby polar bear to stop looking cute – impossible! Sam tried to be quiet, but it never worked. He was heard everywhere he went, whereas his friend Nina moved around like a hamster in slippers. But both of them were quite small, so they had that in common, at least.

"What are you making?" Sam asked Nina,

who was knitting as she walked along. (Yes, really.)

"A new woolly dummy for Nigel," said Nina, her needles moving in a super-fast blur. Nigel was Nina's baby brother, and he liked chewing a knitted dummy, making it more and more spitty with every chomp – nice!

"Lucky Nigel," said Sam. "Did you do your Tudor homework?" he asked. "Henry VIII's wives, remember? What a big fat nightmare!"

Sam sighed (which sounded more like a roar) and shook his head. His messy blond hair rippled like a Golden Retriever shaking itself after a swim. Sam's mum was a hairdresser at Topside's best salon, Prime Cuts, but somehow she never found time to cut her own son's hair.

"I gave each wife a food name to help me remember," Sam said. "Catherine of Tarragon, Ham Boleyn, Jane Sweetcorn. . . But I only got as far as Anne of Cheese. Too many wives!"

Nina nodded and looked serious. She often looked serious. And she sometimes spoke in riddles, like an ancient know-it-all Zen master from mystical times.

"Well, you know what they say, Sam?" said Nina. "Many chips, much salt."

"Exactly," said Sam, even though he had no idea what Nina was on about. "It's OK, though. Mr Clod never minds if I haven't done my homework. He doesn't even mind my loud—"

Sam paused. A movement had caught his eye. It was a small boy, darting along on his little mini legs, and running quickly towards – HOLY ARCTIC-ROLLY! – a busy road. Where were his mum and dad? Had nobody seen him? No! The speeding tot was on a solo mission for a mash-up. Sam saw all this in a second, but there was no time to run to the child as he was too far away. The word DANGER flashed up in bright red capital letters in Sam's mind. Flash! Flash! Flash! And that was it. Without hesitating, Sam shouted:

"STOP!"

STOP

It was no ordinary shout, though. Sam had just created the loudest, most earth-shaking shout ever. It was like a vocal volcano blowing its top. *Boom!* Even Sam was surprised. This was a shout like no shout he had ever made before – and Sam had made some serious noise in his ten years on the planet. It seemed to come from deep inside his body, as if there was a secret chamber of shouts hidden there and he had found the key and released them all in one massive explosion of sound. How loud was it? Impossible to say, but imagine if someone had fitted speakers to Sam and turned the volume up to eleven. That. Timesed by ten.

The child stopped, of course. But so did the cars. And passers-by. And dogs out for a walk. And a line of ants going about their anty business. For almost half a mile around, everybody and anybody stopped and stared in Sam's direction.

"Sorry," said Sam, as quietly as possible.

The child's mother came running towards Sam, her little boy in her arms, shouting, "thank you, thank you!"

Sam felt embarrassed.

"You saved my son," said the mother. "Who knows what would have happened if you hadn't been here? You're a hero!"

A crowd had gathered now, and they all

began clapping and patting Sam on the shoulder and saying things like "good job" and "well done". A Japanese tourist, who happened to be passing, took several photos of Sam, and somebody let off a couple of party poppers while a little dog ran around on his back legs with his front paws in the air. Marvellous stuff!

Sam felt a bit pleased. He didn't know what to say. "Wow," he managed, once he and Nina had walked away. "That was a bit weird. I didn't mean to yell like that. I'm normally loud, but that was super loud!"

Sam had never guessed there was such a mega, ultra-loud voice within him.

"You stopped that child from getting hurt," said Nina, "by using your voice. It was utterly awesome, Sam!"

Suddenly, Sam felt a teensy bit special. Maybe his loud voice could do more than irritate people on a daily basis. That would certainly make a nice change. And being called a hero? Well, he could definitely get used to that.

Chapter 2

INTRODUCING THE MANN

A few minutes later, Sam and Nina walked through the big iron gates of their school. It was a chunky old Victorian building, with high ceilings, shady staircases up to forgotten floors and even a bomb shelter under the playground, left over from the war. It's quite possible it hadn't been decorated since then either. The lemon-yellow paint in the classrooms was flaking off. But who cares about a peeling paint-job? Sam and

Nina loved school and all their teachers too, including the head teacher, Mrs Brisket.

And here she was, standing in Sam's classroom with Miss Hash, the school secretary beside her, holding a clipboard and ready to take notes if notes were needed.

"I'm sorry to tell you, children, that Mr Clod has left Topside Junior School," said Mrs Brisket, gripping the old-fashioned ear trumpet she used to help her hear. "All rather sudden, but we are extremely fortunate that Mrs Mann has stepped in at short notice. She will be teaching you from now on. Please give her a warm welcome."

The children looked around, confused.

Where was their teacher?

"Now, where on earth did she get to?" asked Mrs Brisket.

Suddenly, from under the desk, a tall, pale woman with large hands appeared, popping up like a jack-in-the-box. A jack-in-the-box wearing a grey cardigan with massive pockets.

The children gasped.

"I was adjusting my hair," said Mrs Mann, to explain her under-the-desk-ness.

And what hair! It was grey and styled upwards, like a bun gone ballistic. Sam asked his mum about it later, and she said that style was called a beehive. Whether there were any bees living in it was unclear, but it certainly could have housed some insects or even a family of bats, as well as various knick-knacks. It was a massive pillar of hair.

The children stared at Mrs Mann, feeling uneasy. Mrs Mann smiled back at them. It was a thin smile; the sort of smile a disappointed lizard might make. Her eyes roamed slowly over the students, as if she were sizing them up.

"Yes, Sam?" said Mrs Brisket. Sam had raised his hand.

"Would Mrs Mann like me to show her round the school?" Sam said, in his characteristically loud voice. It boomed off the classroom walls and rattled the blinds. "I could even take her down to the bomb shelter, couldn't I? It's awesome down there, Mrs Mann – a bit creepy and you'd have to watch your hair as the roof's a bit low, but. . ."

Sam trailed off. Mrs Mann's mouth had fallen open, like a giant cave of shock, and her eyes were wide with alarm and anger. She did *not* look pleased.

"That won't be necessary," the new teacher replied. "And speak more quietly when you address a teacher."

"Sam is blessed with quite a loud voice," explained Mrs Brisket. "I rather enjoy it, being a bit hopeless on the hearing front!"

She laughed loudly and winked at Sam, before noticing Mrs Mann's unimpressed face.

"We do encourage Sam to be quiet," said

Mrs Brisket, "but no luck so far! I'm sure you'll grow to love his voice."

Mrs Mann wore an expression that said, *I seriously doubt that.*

"I won't tolerate loud voices in this class," Mrs Mann said quietly. "No shouting, no chatting, no laughing, no singing, no chanting, no yodelling, no humming."

"No what-what?" asked Mrs Brisket, lifting her trumpet to her ear.

Mrs Mann turned to the whiteboard and wrote – NO NOISE!

Sam gulped nervously. He couldn't do "no noise". It just wasn't his style. The other children looked worried, too. School, it seemed, was about to get seriously serious, thanks to a woman with a hatred of noise, peculiar hair and a grey cardigan with deep pockets.

Chapter 3
BIG MOUTH STRIKES AGAIN

The children sat quietly as Mrs Mann took the register. There were several names before Sam's: Aaron Abacus and Agatha Ackerbilk, annoying Jeremy Fortesque Winterflunkett – who was frightfully well spoken and thought everyone was beneath him – and Nina. When it came to Sam, he tried to say "here" in an especially quiet voice. But Sam couldn't do quiet, let alone *especially* quiet. Instead, Sam's answer came out loud. He tried to muffle it and as a result, his "here" turned into "here-ullggg". It sounded like a rhino swallowing a jelly. Mrs Mann glowered.

After the register, Mrs Mann got the children to move the desks. Instead of cosy groups of four, they had to put them in twos, all facing the front. Sam was told to sit at the back.

"The greater the distance between your voice and my ears, the better," said Mrs Mann, but otherwise she hardly spoke to the children. Not like their old teacher, Mr Clod, who loved to ramble on about his exotic past working as a ski instructor in Mongolia and a cheese carver in Canada.

Next, it was time for singing assembly in the big hall. Sam was about to sit next to Nina when Mrs Mann stopped him.

"You'll be singing over here, today," she said, steering Sam towards the kitchen next to the hall. "We don't want you to drown out the other children."

The kitchen always smelled of boiled cabbage, even though cabbage was only on the menu on Wednesdays (Windy Wednesdays, as they were nicknamed). Sam glanced around. There was a big metal tub of greyish water on the counter next to him, with some pale hot dogs bobbing about in it. Sam gulped in a queasy way. He peered out through the serving hatch as the school song began:

"We are all shining stars,
We don't need flashy cars,
To feel special. . ."

Sam sighed. It was hard to feel special when you were standing next to a vat of cold hot dogs. Sam *had* felt special at the beginning of the day, when he'd saved the little boy, but that feeling was draining away now, thanks to his new teacher.

After assembly, the children had to read to Mrs Mann. When it came to Sam's turn, Mrs Mann put on a pair of ear muffs to protect her from his loud voice. They had an extra-long strap to fit over her giant hair stack. She looked pretty silly. It would have been funny, except for the fact that it wasn't funny. Instead, Sam felt embarrassed.

"Did I mention that I hate noise?" asked Mrs Mann, staring at him with her tiny mean eyes.

Yeah, I kind of got that, thought Sam. But, wisely, he said nothing.

Later, everyone went outside for athletics. A bunch of Sam's classmates were running the one hundred metres. Sam cheered as his friends zoomed by.

Oh dear.

Don't cheer, Sam!

Oh, you just did.

That sound – like thirty bears yelling at a football match – that was you. The runners stopped in fright. Jeremy Fortesque Winterflunkett fell flat out on his back, stunned. The race had to be started again.

"Sorry," said Sam.

Everyone heard his apology. Everyone always heard Sam. Like that time he shouted BINGO! so loudly during a game that Agatha Ackerbilk fell off her chair. Or that time he played a lion in the class's Safari Show and made all the children in the front row pee their pants when he roared. And that time he auditioned for the school choir and Mrs Mince, the music teacher, was off sick for three days afterwards.

This time, the PE teacher, Mr Rump (bald head, shiny tracksuit, called everyone "son" – even the girls) told Sam to go and help with the long jump.

"Try to put a sock in it too, son," Mr Rump added.

But over at the long jump, Sam couldn't contain his enthusiasm. Each time a classmate bombed down the track and prepared to take one giant leap for mankind, Sam would shout, "Jump!" or "Go!"

It made the children jump, sure, but not in a long-jump way. Startled by Sam's top-volume voice, they pinged off the track like they had been Tasered.

"Sorry," said Sam.

"Right, son, how about going to watch the hurdles?" suggested Mr Rump. "And Sam? Zip it!"

Sam tried to zip it, but as his friends were about to leap the first hurdle, he whispered, **"GO, GO, GO!"** But a whisper from Sam Lowe wasn't like a whisper from anyone else. It wasn't whispery, it was top-volumey! The sound banged against the children's heads like a big bong on a gong. Instead of leaping the hurdles, they crashed into them and fell in a messy heap on the track.

When the children untangled themselves they were annoyed.

"Sam put us off, sir," said Jock Wilson.

Jock was the sportiest boy in the school, and the best at acting and maths and all sorts of other stuff. He said "excellent" a lot, because life, for him, really was excellent and he was excellent too. Nothing was a problem for Jock and he was super positive about everything. Everyone wanted to be friends with him; even the children who didn't really like him. He hardly noticed Sam, though. Sam wasn't really very sporty, or very anything (except loud). The two boys didn't have much in common.

Mr Rump was about to speak when there was a shrill whistle, and everyone turned to see Mrs Mann, who had appeared as if from nowhere. She tucked the whistle back into her upright hairdo and then spoke quietly to Sam.

"Run back to the sports hall and fetch the

school stopwatch," she said.

It took Sam ages to find the watch. Mrs Mann had not been very clear about its location. By the time Sam made it back on to the field, the lesson was over.

Nina appeared at his side. She patted his arm and smiled.

"Bob's Your Uncle?" Nina said. Or rather asked.

Sam understood her mysterious words and, after lunch, the two friends headed up a quiet staircase until they arrived at a door at the very top of the school.

Chapter 4
BOB'S YOUR UNCLE

The door belonged to the room, which belonged to the school caretaker, Bob. Bob was also Sam's uncle. Uncle Bob or, as Sam and Nina knew him, Bob's Your Uncle.

Bob had worked at Topside Junior School for over twenty years. His last name was Rodeo. With a name like that, Bob had wanted to be a cowboy, but he quickly realized there were not many cowboy jobs going in Topside, so he became a caretaker instead. He didn't actually do much work, though. Instead, he spent much of his day either in the staff room or in this room – or his "office" as he liked to call it – drinking tea and listening to his radio, but nobody seemed to mind. They all loved Bob.

"Well now, how are you two today?" asked Bob's Your Uncle when Sam and Nina appeared.

"We're OK," Sam said dejectedly. "Well actually we've got this new teacher, Mrs Mann, and she really hates noise, which is absolutely no good for me."

As Sam spoke, he tried not to stare at Bob's enormous woolly eyebrows. If you stared at

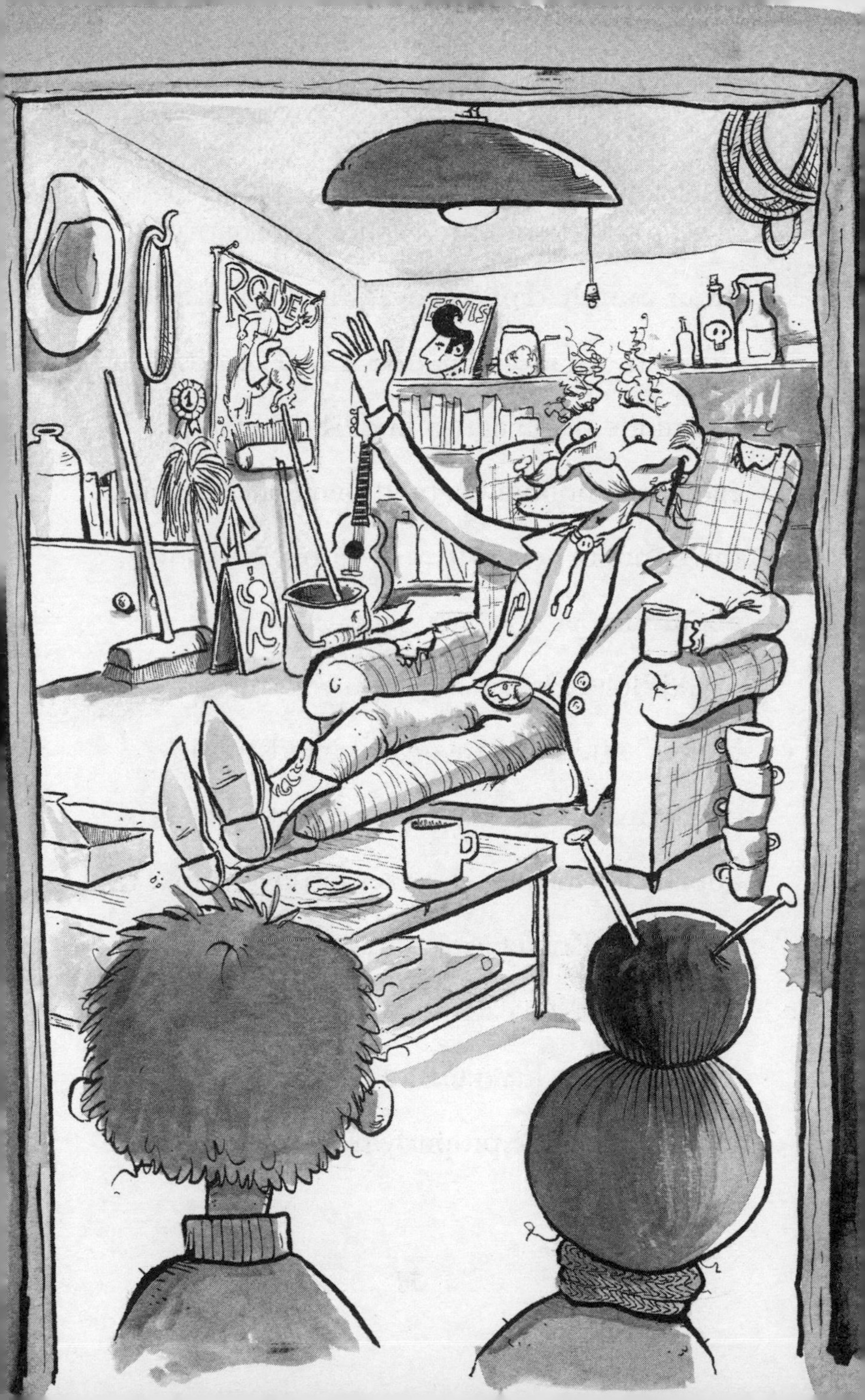
RODEO
ELVIS

them too long you sometimes saw shapes in them. Sam had once seen a unicorn in Bob's left eyebrow and Nina had seen a comet that seemed to travel across both. Some people even thought that his eyebrows could predict the future or reveal truths. Sam wasn't sure about that.

"Ah yes. Mrs Sandy Mann with the giant hands!" said Bob, waving his hands at the children and chuckling. "Mr Rump said she's applied for the head teacher job. You know, when Mrs Brisket leaves at the end of the year."

The children exchanged worried looks. Mrs Mann as head teacher of Topside Junior School would be properly pants news. With her in charge, every single child in the school would have to play by her no-fun rules, and that spelled disaster for happiness and nice times. Bob noticed Sam and Nina looking concerned. "Not a fan of Mrs Mann?" he asked. "She's probably all right, but I'll keep my ears open when I'm in the staff room and let you know if I hear anything about her. Cup of tea?"

The children said no thanks. This happened every time they visited Bob's Your Uncle. He offered tea. They said no thanks. That was just the way it was.

As they were leaving, Bob pointed at a door on the other side of the landing.

"That reminds me," he said. "I thought I saw Mrs Mann up here at the start of the day. It looked like she had just come out of that storeroom, but nobody has used it for years so, no, I must have been mistaken. It was early and I was half asleep!"

"Can we look inside it?" asked Sam.

"You could if I had the key!" said Bob. "But I've lost it. It's usually safe on the key chain I keep in my pocket. Funny, really. I can't work out how it just magically disappeared."

Uncle Bob frowned and his massive eyebrows came together like a huge woolly hedge.

"I tried looking through the keyhole, but my

eyesight's not wonderful and I couldn't make out a thing," Bob added.

So Sam had a look. He squinted through the keyhole. It took a while for his eyes to adjust to the gloom. At first he couldn't see anything, but then he made out a shape on the floor. It was covered in a blanket and there were two shoes poking out. Boots actually, just the kind worn by. . .

"Mr Clod!" screamed Sam, super loud,

making Bob's eyebrows ping up and down like a bouncy ball in a box. "There is somebody in there, and I think it's Mr Clod!"

Sam tried the door, rattling the handle, but sure enough it was shut tight.

"Quick," he said, grabbing Nina's hand. "We need to tell Mrs Brisket."

And the two friends raced downstairs.

Chapter 5
CALLING MR CLOD

At the bottom of the stairs, Sam turned a corner and crashed into Mr Rump – "Careful, son!" – before rushing to see the head teacher.

Mrs Brisket listened carefully as Sam explained how he thought Mr Clod was locked in the storeroom at the top of the school.

"I understand your concern, Sam," said Mrs Brisket, "but I'm quite sure Mr Clod is fine and not trapped in a cupboard or a storeroom or anywhere. If it makes you happy,

I'll ring him to check. Now return to your classroom or Mrs Mann will wonder where you are."

Back in class, Sam had no time to puzzle over what he had seen, as Mrs Mann called him straight over to her desk. Jock Wilson was standing there as well.

"You two can be the first to groom Hugo," said Mrs Mann.

She pointed at a furry toy cat sitting on her desk – Hugo. Sam looked at Hugo. He seemed rather lifelike, and then Sam realized with a gulp that Hugo was not a soft toy at all. Hugo was a stuffed cat. Or a cat that had been stuffed. However you want to look at it.

"Hugo is my cat," said Mrs Mann, turning to Sam and smiling. "*Was* my cat. . . He used to be such a noisy nuisance. Always meowing. I enjoy his company much more now."

Mrs Mann gazed at the cat. The cat, with his quiet glass eyes, gazed back. Sam shuddered a bit.

"Jock, you can brush Hugo's hair, and Sam, you buff his whiskers," said Mrs Mann, handing them a comb and a cloth.

The two boys began their unusual task, glancing at each other in a "Can you believe this? No I can't either" kind of way. Sam and Jock never normally worked together but now here they were, teamed up to clean and groom a stuffed cat. They had only been combing and buffing for a little while when they heard a sound. It was a phone ringing very quietly, but it had an unusual ringtone – the sound of African drums. More peculiar still, it was coming from Mrs Mann's head. The boys watched as she darted her hand into her tower of hair, rummaged about and then silenced the phone. Jock and Sam glanced at each other. If they could have had speech bubbles above their heads, they would have been full of exclamation marks. The two boys knew what they had heard and when school was over, they rushed outside and both said, at the same time:

"That was Mr Clod's phone!"

For, yes, that unique ringtone belonged to Mr Clod's phone. "Reminds me of that time I worked as a wildebeest herder in Kenya," Mr Clod had told the children.

Nina caught up with the boys as Jock asked, "Why does Mrs Mann have Mr Clod's phone?"

Sam wasn't sure. His mind was racing, trying to piece all the facts together. And he was distracted by standing so close to Jock. Him and Jock. Sharing a problem. Chatting. This had never happened before! Nina came to Sam's rescue.

"We think Mr Clod is trapped in a storeroom upstairs!" said Nina, filling Jock in.

"Perhaps Mrs Mann has something to do with it!" said Sam, who was so excited and agitated that he was beginning to shout.

"What?" said Jock. Sam gulped. Perhaps Jock would laugh at Sam when he began to explain; go off to play sport with the sporty kids. But no! Jock was intrigued.

"Go on," said Jock, taking Sam seriously.

Sam felt a little pulse of pride – he had Jock's full attention. He explained how he had seen a person-shaped shape lying in the cupboard with boots just like the ones Mr Clod wore, and then about how Bob's Your Uncle had lost the key to the storeroom, but thought he had seen Mrs Mann up there. And now they knew that she had Mr Clod's phone too. In her hair! It all looked fishy – fishier than a coach-load of cod on their way to the aquarium.

"Maybe she stole the key to the storeroom off Bob, somehow," said Sam. "Then she put Mr Clod in there."

"Why doesn't he try to get out?" asked Jock. "If it was me, I'd try to break the door down or dig a tunnel or something else really excellent and brave."

"He looked fast asleep," Sam explained.

"Maybe you can wake him," chipped in Nina. "With your super-loud voice. Just like this morning when you stopped that boy from running into the road. Really yell!"

"Yes, you're a bit of a shouter, aren't you," said Jock. "Excellent – let's try it."

The three children sneaked back inside and up the stairs to the storeroom. Jock peered through the keyhole and then sprang back, looking shocked. "It's him! It's definitely Mr Clod," gasped Jock. "I can see his face, but he's asleep."

The children tried the door again. Still locked.

"Shout at him, Sam!" said Nina.

Sam nodded, took a big breath and then roared through the keyhole.

"MR CLOD!!!!"

Jock and Nina shrank back from the noise, but the sleeping figure did not stir.

"TIME TO WAKE UP!!!"

Mr Clod did nothing.

"It's no good," said Sam. "He can't hear me."

But someone else had. Suddenly, Mrs Mann appeared. Uh-oh!

"Whatever you think you're doing, stop doing it. Whatever you think you saw, you didn't. Whatever you imagine you know, you don't. Understand?" she said, staring at each child hard in turn. "If I catch you up here again, I will punish you good and properly. Now go home."

Chapter 6

THE HILLS ARE ALIVE WITH THE SOUND OF SHOUTING

Sam, Nina and Jock walked silently away from school.

"Maybe if I could just shout a tiny bit louder," said Sam, "I could wake Mr Clod up and we could ask him what happened."

"Perfect," said Jock. "Let's practise up at the country park where there's no one around. I've got basketball now, but call me later."

"But I don't have a phone yet!" Sam protested.

"Call me with your *voice*," said Jock. "I only

live three streets away. Bet I'll hear you!"

"Oh yes, yes and triple yes!" said Nina excitedly. "Jock's right – we don't need phones when we have your voice, Sam!"

Sam wasn't sure about this, but later that evening, he went up to his room and shouted:

"NINA! MEET ME AT THE BOTTOM OF YOUR ROAD. WEAR YOUR HAT THAT'S SHAPED LIKE A LIGHTHOUSE."

That's a good test, thought Sam. *Now I will see whether she really heard me.*

Sam ran round to Nina's road. Soon he spotted movement in the distance. A yellow blob on a stripy red-and-white column was bobbing his way. It was the lighthouse hat; the one Nina had knitted herself. And underneath it? Nina's head! And underneath that? The whole rest of Nina!

"You heard me!" Sam boomed. In his excitement, his volume had gone right up.

Across the street, a toddler threw his ice-cream cone into the air in shock and it landed on his dad's head like a small, creamy hat.

"Now call Jock," said Nina. "He lives further away, but you can do it!"

So Sam called Jock in his big, ear-bending voice. Shocked by the sound, a young woman out jogging started running around in circles, confused and shaken. Never mind about that, though, because seconds later Jock arrived wearing a tracksuit and carrying a stopwatch.

"Excellent," said Jock. "Now let's practise in the park. We can run there – it'll be fun. Pick it up now, let's go!"

Sam was panting like a hot dog in a heatwave by the time he got to the park. Nina handed Jock some earplugs she had just knitted, and they waited for Sam to catch his breath and shout.

First, Sam let loose his super-extra-loud voice, the one he had used to save a little boy that morning.

"HELLO!" he shouted.

Jock and Nina covered their ears. Even with the earplugs in, the sound was enormous. Jock gave the thumbs up. Nina clapped.

"If that doesn't wake up Mr Clod, I don't know what will," she said.

Sam grinned. This felt fun. More fun than

watching pig racing. More fun than punching custard. More fun than last year's Topside Festival of Fun, which everyone agreed had been the best in the town's history.

"I AM AWESOME," Sam yelled next. **"I RULE!"**

The words flew up to the clouds and

bounced off the distant hills. When he shouted, everything seemed to shake. It was super-powerful shouting. Jock and Nina whooped and high-fived each other. By crumpets, this boy could yell!

"BIG FAT MANGO FUZZPOPS!" yelled Sam.

Jock and Nina collapsed into giggles. Sam laughed too. He felt great! He felt

tall and strong and mighty for the first time in his life (even though he was actually short and skinny and not at all mighty).

"Excellent!" said Jock. "Really massively excellent! Now rest that voice. Big day tomorrow – you need to wake Mr Clod up so we can set him free. Then we can work out what in the name of nuttiness is going on."

Chapter 7

SAM'S MUM HAS SOME NEWS

When Sam got home from the park, he was feeling excited. With his new, super-loud voice in shape, he felt confident he could wake Mr Clod.

Sam's mum was sitting at the kitchen table when he got in.

"I've been speaking to your teacher, Mrs Mann," she said.

Oh dear. Sam was used to conversations like this. He knew how they usually went.

Something to do with his teacher being concerned about his loudness, blah, blah. . .

"Your teacher is concerned about your loudness," said his mum.

There you go, thought Sam.

His mum continued, "She said you were yelling at top volume in the school today and she suggested you see a speech therapist. So I have made an appointment for you tomorrow morning."

"Tomorrow?" Sam boomed.

His mum ducked, as if the shout was going to knock her over. Sam couldn't go tomorrow morning; he had to save Mr Clod. No time for speech therapy!

"Mrs Mann says it's urgent that we tackle your voice," said Sam's mum. "Maybe she's right. You know I love you the way you are (although I really *must* cut your hair), but you might be happier if you were less loud."

No chance, thought Sam. OK, his voice got him into trouble at school sometimes, but he was just beginning to explore what it could do. Being able to shout super loud and call Nina and Jock from his house was exciting, *and* he had stopped that little boy from being squished too. Now he had an even bigger job to do – saving Mr Clod. *No*, Sam thought, *for the first time in my life I am happy with my voice. I don't want to be quiet.* Anyone could be quiet, after all – there was nothing amazing about that. Being loud on the other hand? Well, that was just starting to get interesting!

Chapter 8

SAM'S APPOINTMENT

In the morning, Sam called Nina from his bedroom again. She was in her room working on a new project (knitted bookshelves) but raced round to see him. Sam explained how he had an appointment with a speech therapist.

"But I'll be back in school around lunchtime," he told Nina. "We can go straight up to the storeroom and try to bust Mr Clod out."

Then Sam had to go. He felt nervous while

his mum drove him to his appointment. He didn't know what to expect, except perhaps half an hour of something stupid, annoying, annoyingly stupid or even stupidly annoying.

Sam's mum told the lady at the front desk that Sam was here and then, ruffling his hair, she left to go to work. "Good luck!" she said, cheerfully. She could see that Sam was nervous.

Sam sat down in a deep armchair and stared at some fish swimming around a tank and then at the speech therapist's door. There was a sign on it saying BRYCE CANYON. Nothing more.

"You can go in now,' said the receptionist

lady after a while, smiling at Sam, so in
he went.

Entering the room, he saw a man standing behind a desk. He looked the complete opposite of how Sam had imagined a speech therapist might look. He was tall, with a scar down one cheek, and he wore sunglasses and a long black leather jacket, even though it was nice and warm indoors.

"Hello, Sam, I'm Bryce Canyon," he said. His voice was deep with a soft American accent. He indicated a chair and Sam sat down.

"OK," said the man. "Show me what you've got."

Sam didn't understand. Wasn't the man going to chat a bit? Ask Sam what the problem was?

"Show me what you can do," said Mr Canyon. "With your voice. I think there is some volume in there, so c'mon. Loud as you like."

Sam cleared his throat.

"Hello!" he said. It was loud, but nothing to wet your pants over.

Bryce Canyon shook his head.

"More," he said.

"GOOD MORNING," Sam shouted, at a volume that can only be described as "extremely loud". Think workmen drilling up a pavement in a hurricane.

"Not bad," said Mr Canyon, folding his arms. "But I think you can do better."

Right you are then, thought Sam. *You asked for it.* This time he let rip.

"AAARRRGGHHHHHH!"

Bryce Canyon rocked back on his heels as Sam's biggest super-loud voice tore past. Pencils skittered across the desk, a window was hurled open, and outside, a window cleaner fell off his ladder in shock and landed in a bucket of water.

"Nice," said Bryce Canyon, adjusting his glasses.

Sam couldn't believe it. Nice! What? Not "shush!" or "silence!" or "quiet, Sam!".

Bryce Canyon sat down and leaned across his desk.

"What you have here is a gift," he said. "This voice of yours is a powerful tool; a mighty weapon but you must learn to master it and use it wisely. There may come a time when you can do great things with your voice; when your voice can help innocent people. But first, you must learn to control it, see?"

Sam wasn't sure that he did see, and was about to ask a question, but Bryce looked at his watch.

"Time's up," he said. "See you tomorrow. And take this, Sam."

Bryce handed Sam a comic book. "See what this guy gets up to," he said. "From zero to hero! It's quite a story. And remember what I told you."

Chapter 9
CAUGHT NAPPING

It was just after lunch when Sam got back to school. The halls were quiet – everyone was in class. He was mulling over what Bryce Canyon had said as he stepped through the door of his classroom. Which is why it took him a moment to clock what was happening inside.

Sam's classmates were all *asleep*! Spark out! In the land of nod! Every one of them had their heads on their desks, still and quiet and sleeping like puppies that have been partying for a day and a half. There was Mrs Mann, too, leaning over a big map that was spread across her desk.

Sam only had a second to take in this strange scene before Mrs Mann saw him and shot towards the door, holding her cardigan out to the sides to block Sam's view, like a giant lady-teacher-bird swooping down.

"You will read in the library until the bell goes," she said, hurrying Sam up the corridor.

"Can't I get my water bottle?" Sam asked, looking back towards the classroom.

He didn't want a drink, though; he wanted a look at what the heck was happening in there. Had Mrs Mann reached new levels of boringness, causing the whole class to fall asleep? Or was there more to it than that?

"Use the drinking fountain," said Mrs

Mann. "And stay in the library. Or else."

Sam didn't like the idea of "or else". Sounded a bit worrying. So he sat down and took the comic that Bryce had given him out of his bag. It was called, *The Astonishing Col Slaw*. Quickly, Sam was drawn in as humble Colin Slawbert, who had fallen into a vat of grated cabbage on a trip round a veg factory, turned into the mighty superhero Col Slaw, blasting out the salady side-dish from his hands to defeat baddies. Go, Col!

Sam was so involved in Col Slaw's escapades, as the young hero learned to manage his mighty cabbage power, that he forgot all about Bryce Canyon. And about

Mr Clod in the storeroom upstairs. And his knocked-out classmates. . . Until the bell went and he hurried outside.

There they were, stumbling on to the street, woolly and woozy and barely awake. Sam had never seen anything like it. It was a scene of utter, utter chaos.

Jock, usually so energetic, was dragging himself along like he was wearing concrete trousers, while Nina was wilting like a flower without water. Agatha Ackerbilk walked into a tree, bounced off it and collapsed against a wheelie bin, while Jeremy Fortesque Winterflunkett draped himself over his dog, Mallory, who trotted up the pavement with the fast-asleep kid hanging off him.

This was so bonkers, it was almost funny – until Sam realized his friends were in danger.

Some of them were trying to skateboard or ride scooters as usual, while still half asleep. Sam watched his classmates wobble and wibble and mumble and muddle. He saw them wander dangerously close to the road, slip on pavements, trip over kerbs, collide with trees and prang into parking meters, while bewildered parents shrieked in alarm and panicked car drivers blasted their horns. This was serious.

Sam bit his lip, unsure what to do, when he heard Bryce Canyon's voice in his head, like the speech therapist had gone mini and climbed in there for a chat. *Your voice is a gift*, said the Bryce inside Sam's brain.

Use it for good, Sam!

"Of course!" said Sam, pulling himself together, "and it's time to share my gift with the world!"

Sam got off to a good start. A few super-noisy **"STOPS"** and he had prevented Aaron Abacus from scooting into a skip full of old radiators. Instead he collapsed into a dozing heap. Then Sam saw Jock reaching sleepily for his bike!

"NO, JOCK!" yelled Sam, but despite Sam's top-volume trumpeting, Jock hardly seemed to hear Sam and began to cycle shakily up the street.

This was not good, but not good was about

to turn into *really* not good. Sam spotted people leaving Topside Hall at the end of the road. It was the Topside Community Custard Club, finishing their monthly Custard Cook-Up. Uh-oh! There was a lady holding a huge tub of custard and – gadzooks! – Jock was pedalling straight for her.

Sam called out again, but it was too late. *Whack!* went Jock, colliding with the lady.

"Aarrgggahhh!" went the lady, dropping her tub.

Splosh! went the custard, a great tidal wave of yellow spilling over Jock and down the road. It was a custard-astrophe!

Meanwhile, other Custard Club members, unaware of what was happening, were getting into their cars. Sam stared in horror. They were about to drive straight towards the sleepy children. Too dangerous!

"NO, NO, NO, NO, NO,"

Sam yelled, running towards the hall.

Then everything happened very quickly. Sam was shouting at the people to stay back, but they didn't understand. Then, before Sam really knew what he was doing, he stopped shouting and hummed instead, like a gigantic, all-powerful fridge.

MMMWAARRRGGHHH!

The humungous hum came from deep in

his chest and burst forwards like a tsunami of sound. You could *see* Sam's voice. It moved like shock waves from an explosion, blasting everything in its path. The mighty wave rocketed up the street, the force rattling windows as it barrelled forwards, and then – *BOOM!* – it pinned the Custard Clubbers to the hall wall and even ripped off one man's hair. Really? Yes! For this man wore a wig – or he did, until Sam blasted it clean into the air like a flying hairy cowpat.

Panicking a little, Sam let out another booming bounce, hoping to force the children back into the playground where they would be safe. Instead, the blast picked up a wheelie bin, and Sam watched in horror as it flew through the air . . . straight towards Nina!

"NINAAAAA!" yelled Sam.

Nina slowly looked up and her dozy eyes fixed on the bin as it flew over her head – *WHOOOSH!* – just missing her, then – *SMASH!* – it whammed into a car windscreen and shattered the glass into fifty besquillion pieces.

WHEEE-WHEEE-WHEEE went the car's alarm in protest, like a toddler having a tantrum over a biscuit.

Sam cringed at the sound, but the other children woke up. Snap – just like that. Wide awake and with it.

At last, the sleepy crisis was over.

Chapter 10
SOME BRYCE ADVICE

Sam felt exhausted and shaken when he got home. What had just happened? And why had what happened, happened? And what else could have happened while all this was happening? These were serious questions. So serious, in fact, that Sam used his big voice to call Nina and Jock to a meeting in his bedroom to discuss the afternoon's strange, sleepy chaos.

Jock and Nina were confused about the

day's events. They remembered answering the register, then the next thing they knew it was the end of the day and they were out on the street with Jock all covered in custard. Sam had to explain how he had seen the class asleep and, later, watched as the half-awake children had stumbled into danger outside the school.

"Maybe we are just falling asleep because Mrs Mann's lessons are so boring," said Jock.

"That doesn't make sense though," said Nina, looking up from her knitting. (She was creating a set of reusable knitted teabags for Bob's Your Uncle.) "Surely Mrs Mann would wake us up?"

"What if it's not Mrs Mann's lessons, but Mrs Mann herself?" said Sam, shouting so loudly with excitement that Beef, the dog who lived three doors up, started barking. "She is putting us all to sleep."

"Why?" asked Nina.

"Well, what do we know about Mrs Mann?" said Sam. "She hates noise, right? And a class of children makes a lot of noise, doesn't it? Particularly when I'm in it! Unless. . ."

"Unless every child in the class is *asleep*!" said Nina.

"What about Mr Clod?" asked Jock. "He's spark out in the storeroom. Could Mrs Mann have sent him to sleep, too? But why?"

"We have to wake him up and find out," said Sam.

"How?" asked Nina.

"I'm going to blow the door down!" said Sam.

"What?" said Nina.

"Cool," said Jock.

The two friends didn't yet know about Sam's new shock-wave hum.

"Trust me," said Sam. "I feel different. I'm changing. I'm not that annoying noisy kid any more and I'm tired of trying to keep quiet. I'm large and in charge! And I'm going to take that door out."

Chapter 11

WATCHING AND WAITING

Sam was quiet as he, Nina and Jock walked to school the next day. He didn't want to waste his voice; he needed all his sound and power for a shock wave that would free Mr Clod.

Once at school, the children sneaked indoors but – double-bubble disaster! – found Bob's Your Uncle stretching bright red DO NOT ENTER tape across the stairs.

"You can't go up," said Bob's Your Uncle. "Mrs Mann says she doesn't want people using the stairs. She said she had them examined and they are too wobbly to pass health and safety rules. Funny, though – they seem fine to me."

Bob's huge eyebrows looked confused, as only oversized facial hair can.

The children were not confused, though. They knew what was going on – Mrs Mann was trying to stop them from helping Mr Clod. Sam felt crushed, like last week's banana in the bottom of a backpack. How could he make it upstairs now?

Things did not improve during lessons that morning. Mrs Mann fixed the friends with her beady eyes, which isn't easy to do when there are three children to watch and you only have two eyes, but somehow Mrs Mann managed it.

At lunchtime, Mrs Mann made Sam, Nina and Jock stay inside to tidy up the classroom. She was on to them. The children felt desperate. How could they help Mr Clod with Mrs Mann watching their every move?

The answer was – they couldn't. But their lunchtime of tidying was not a complete waste. Mrs Mann read her chemistry book while Jock and Nina sharpened pencils and Sam dusted around her desk. Sam noticed a large sheet of paper poking out from a drawer. He stared and then, after checking that his teacher was still reading, silently slid the paper out.

It was a map of their town, Topside – the map Sam had seen Mrs Mann looking at yesterday. Sam peered closer. Mrs Mann had circled all the schools and nurseries in the town in red: St Mumpsy's, the Topside Upside Academy, Botty View Primary and Tiny Titch Tot World, the nursery where Nina's little brother Nigel went. What did this mean?

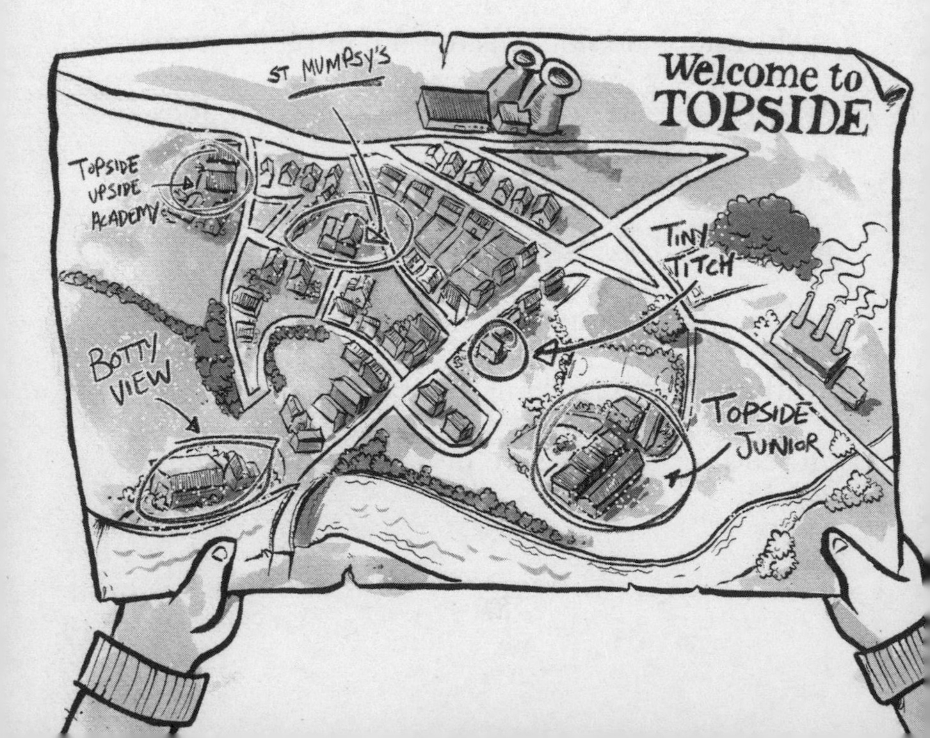

What was Mrs Mann up to? Sam quietly slid the paper back just as the bell rang. There was no time to tell his friends about the map, though; it was time to visit Bryce again.

Chapter 12
MORE BRYCE ADVICE

Sitting in Bryce's office that afternoon, Sam told him all about the sleepy chaos outside school the day before. Bryce wasn't interested in why the children had been so drowsy; he only wanted to know how Sam had reacted. Sam explained that he had helped to divert his friends from danger with his voice, but had also discovered a new force – a kind of shock wave that could move objects.

"I was chucking bins around and blasting

people's wigs off!" said Sam. "It went a bit bonkers."

"It's because you haven't mastered your voice yet," said Bryce.

"Maybe it's too dangerous to use," Sam said. Suddenly, the idea of blowing the door down to Mr Clod's storeroom seemed risky and daft rather than daring.

"Once you have it under control, it won't be," Bryce said. "So how did this whole situation end? Did anybody get hurt?"

"I don't think so," said Sam. "A car alarm went off and the noise seemed to finally bring all the children back to normal."

"Interesting," said Bryce, tapping something

into his laptop. "Watch this, Sam."

Bryce showed Sam some footage of a lyre bird; a big black bird with a frilly tail that lives in Australia. It could imitate twenty different bird species, but it could also mimic other noises with amazing accuracy, including a car alarm.

"Wow!" said Sam as he watched the bird, its long beak opening and closing with each *WOO-WOO* sound.

"You could do that, too," said Bryce. "Train your voice, Sam, and teach it new sounds. Make it work for you – and for good. Let me know how you get on."

Chapter 13

SOUNDING THE ALARM

On his walk back to school, Sam heard a car alarm, coming from a fancy sports car parked by the road. He listened hard, walked on a little and hid behind some bushes to try to imitate the sound. **"WHEEEE-WHEEEE-WHEEEE,"** he went.

Easy! He got it like that. The ear-bashing volume. The nasty tinny sound. Done.

Next, he decided to try it on location. Yesterday's accident with his shock wave and the bin had taught him that he needed to practise. Doing his car alarm in the park wasn't enough. He had to test it in a real situation.

Sam saw a fancy office block with a car park full of posh cars. He crouched behind a wall and let rip a loud, shrill car-alarm call.

Seconds later, a businessman in a suit raced out of the office. When he realized his car was fine, he looked around in confusion, before heading back inside.

As the man got through the front door, Sam did the car alarm again.

"What?" said the man, who came running out a second time. He checked his car, then back he went.

"WHEEEE-WHEEEE-WHEEEE," went Sam for a third time. Out came the man again, like he was on a

piece of elastic.

Sam could hardly contain his giggles. This was hilarious!

Feeling brave, Sam created a different car alarm. More of a **"WAARRPP-WAARRPP"** than a **"WHEEEE-WHEEEE"**. This worked too. A woman came trotting out of the building, looking worried, her keys jingling. Sam's cheeks ached from grinning. This was like whistling for a dog!

Sam let out a few more car alarms, making the woman scurry in and out, and then he slipped silently away. Sam now understood what Bryce meant about training his voice, but if he could perfect his car-alarm call in one morning, surely it wouldn't take too much work to get his shock wave under control and maybe learn a bunch of other cool sounds too. Ready to help the children next time they went to sleep. Ready to save Mr Clod. If only he could get upstairs. . .

Chapter 14

SAM SUSPECTS. . .

Walking to school the next morning, Nina was busy knitting a new set of gloveless fingers – the opposite of fingerless gloves – as she told Sam about a letter the head teacher had sent round to the parents the day before.

"It said we had to go to bed earlier," said Nina. "Mrs Brisket thinks we're staying up too late and that's why we fell asleep in class and got into danger."

Sam shook his head.

"I know Mrs Mann is involved and I'm worried her plans stretch far beyond our class," Sam said. "I found a map in her desk with all the schools in the area marked on it. It even had Nigel's nursery on it!"

"Not Tiny Titch Tot World?" said Nina, her hands pausing on her knitting needles for a second. "Is Nigel in danger?"

"Maybe," said Sam, "but try not to worry. I'm going to get Mr Clod out. He may have information that will help us, so we can protect ourselves and other children too."

In class, Mrs Mann sat quietly at her desk while the children worked. Sam watched her. Everything was peaceful, until, suddenly, the sound of the school fire-alarm ripped through the air.

It was an ear-shredding, rattling bell of an alarm, louder than usual and enough to joggle your brains about. It seemed to be coming from the back of the room, near Sam, which was strange, but no one noticed. They were all too shocked by the noise, particularly Mrs Mann, who was wearing a look of total horror. Her eyebrows had shot up and nearly disappeared into her hair. She jumped up and began ushering the children out quickly. Everyone wanted to get out to the playground, too, where it was safe and much quieter.

Mrs Mann led the children outside, and in

the crush, Sam, Nina and Jock broke free of their classmates, quietly ducked under the DO NOT ENTER tape that blocked off the stairs, and raced up.

"Top work, Sam!" said Jock, high-fiving him as they galloped towards the storeroom.

"When did you learn to do that?" asked Nina.

Sam shrugged modestly and said he'd been practising. After mastering a car alarm it was an easy step up to the school fire-alarm. Now the whole school would be out in the playground for the next ten minutes or so, giving Sam, Nina and Jock a chance to rescue Mr Clod.

"Stand back," said Sam, in front of the storeroom door. Then, without a moment's hesitation, Sam began to hum. Jock and Nina stared at him.

"Is he going to burp?" asked Jock.

This was no belch, though! The hum grew and grew, like a deep rumble, until – *BOOM!*

Sam released his shock wave and the door exploded inwards – *KERBOOSH!* – like a woolly mammoth had charged it.

"Flipping excellent!" said Jock. Then the children noticed that, despite the explosion, Mr Clod remained asleep. Jock tried to shake him awake and Nina poked him with a knitting needle, but it was no good.

SL

Time for another blast, thought Sam, only this time he would be doing his car alarm.

"Cover your ears," said Sam, and then he was off again, letting out a mighty **WHEEEE-WHEEEE**.

At the sound, Mr Clod's eyelids flickered and then, just like that, he woke up. It had worked!

"Mr Clod!" shouted the children excitedly. "You're awake! You're awake!"

Mr Clod sat up and smiled. "Hello, children," he said, looking puzzled and still very sleepy. "Where are we and why am I on the floor?"

"We think Mrs Mann has put you to sleep

in here," Sam explained.

"Mrs Mann?" said Mr Clod. "I know that name. Big hair, pale face, grey cardigan?"

"That's her," said Jock.

"She used to teach chemistry at the school I worked in before. She was thrown out for doing funny experiments in the lab," said Mr Clod.

"But why did she trap you up here, Mr Clod?" asked Sam.

"No idea!" said Mr Clod. "No offence, but I can't see why someone would be so desperate to teach you lot that they would go to all this bother to get me out of the way."

Everyone fell silent for a moment, thinking

hard. Then they heard the other children in the playground, getting ready to come back inside.

"Time to go," said Sam. "Quick, Mr Clod, let's get you out of here. We'll take you straight to Mrs Brisket's office."

"No!" said Mr Clod. "I need to get home and feed my cat. And have a shower and something to eat. I don't feel very strong. In fact, I feel rather odd. But don't worry, I'll be back soon, once I've sorted myself out."

The children began helping Mr Clod downstairs, but then Sam stopped.

"What's wrong?" asked Nina.

"We need to cover our tracks!" said Sam. "If Mrs Mann notices Mr Clod is gone, she'll be extra suspicious."

So Sam raced back to the storeroom and rearranged the blankets to make it look as though they were covering Mr Clod's body underneath. Then Sam raced off to find Bob's Your Uncle, to ask him to fix the door back on, as soon as he could, so Mrs Mann would never guess.

Finally, Sam caught up with Nina and Jock at the front gate, supporting the wobbly

Mr Clod. Outside in the daylight, they could see that Mr Clod was ill. He looked pale and weak. That's what happens when you have lived in a cupboard for ages. Not good for you. Don't try living in a cupboard at home, kids.

"You better go home and rest, sir," said Sam. "Don't worry. That will give us time to see what Mrs Mann does next. So far, we don't have much evidence against her. We need to understand what her grand plan is."

Mr Clod frowned, nodded and then wobbled away.

Chapter 15

STAY AWAKE – THERE'S LOTS AT STAKE

"So what have we learned?" said Sam on the way home that afternoon.

"We think Mrs Mann is putting us to sleep," said Jock.

"And we reckon she also put Mr Clod to sleep so she could teach our class," added Nina.

"Then there was the map I found on her desk," said Sam.

"Oh yes! With baby Nigel's nursery on it,"

said Nina, looking worried and then cross. "She must not harm my baby brother!"

"That makes me think she has plans for the other schools in our area," said Sam. "Perhaps she wants to put the children in them to sleep too."

"But how does she do it?" asked Nina.

"I don't know, but I'm going to find out!" shouted Sam. "I plan to spy on her."

"Nice! Excellent!" said Jock enthusiastically. He loved a bit of spying and derring-do.

"Slight problem, though," said Nina. "Next time Mrs Mann puts us to sleep, you'll be asleep too."

"I've thought of that," said Sam. "And I've

got a solution – coffee! I hate the taste, but never mind. I will use the power of caffeine! Hopefully it will help me stay awake long enough to see what Mrs Mann is up to."

Now, *definitely* don't try this at home. Coffee is for grown-ups who stay up late watching TV documentaries about submarines or famous sheep-farmers, and then need to feel awake for work the next day. It's not really for children. Unless you're Sam Lowe and you suspect your teacher is – somehow – sending you and your classmates to sleep deliberately and then failing to wake them up properly, thus putting their lives at risk. Then – and only then – is coffee the secret weapon that just might help you stay awake long enough to discover what in the name of Frappuccinos is going on.

The next day was Friday, the day which almost always follows Thursday. Sitting at the kitchen table that morning, Sam waited for his mum to finish her breakfast.

"I best get ready," she said. "I've got a busy day at the salon: a trim for Katie Kim, then there's Mrs Boots – I'm doing her roots – and a cut-and-colour for Mrs McMuller – her hair's got duller."

Once Sam's mum was upstairs, Sam topped up the coffee pot and guzzled back a cup.

"Blaargghh!" Sam roared. "How can anyone drink this? Tastes disgusting!"

Then, to add a sugar rush to his caffeine buzz, Sam chomped down a handful of wine gums and trousered two lollies to eat on the way to school.

It wasn't long before the caffeine and sugar kicked in. As Sam walked along with Nina, he began to get twitchy. His speech got faster. His eyelids flickered. He could not stop talking.

"The thing is, Nina," he explained, talking very fast indeed. "I feel my voice could help with all this – help everyone in class, and help Mr Clod too. I mean, I know I've not done a brilliant job so far. That wheelie bin hitting the car wasn't great, but I'm still learning, you see, and you have to start somewhere, don't you?"

Sam took a breath and sucked his lolly for a few seconds.

"You know that woman said I was a hero for stopping her child from running into the road the other day?" Sam continued. "Well I'm not saying I'm a hero, but I do think I need a name, you know? I need an identity. To make me feel really proper. I was thinking, my voice *is* me. I used to wish I could be quieter, but I can't. Being loud is who I am – I don't want to say sorry for it any more. I'm not Silent Sam, or The Wordless One, or Quiet Kid. People always say that I'm Super Loud! And you know what? That's fine. That's IT. Geddit? Sam Lowe is SUPER LOUD!"

Nina beamed. She was feeling excited too. As Sam spoke, Nina knitted, her hands seeming to fly extra fast with the needles.

"That sounds great, Sam," she said. "But you must keep your identity secret. At least for now. Mrs Mann must not know what power you have. Don't blow it, Sam. We need you. The school needs you! Nigel and his baby friends at Tiny Titch Tot World nursery need you! The whole of Topside needs you! Your voice can protect us and shout out the truth about Mrs Mann – whatever that turns out to be! So remember this. . .'

And then, grinning, Nina held up a woolly banner she had just knitted.

"YOU CAN'T BAG A WEASEL!" read Sam.

“Ooh, sorry, not that one,” said Nina, rummaging about and finding another banner. Smiling, she waved it at Sam. It said, simply:

WE NEED YOU, SUPER LOUD!

Chapter 16

I SPY WITH MY TWITCHY EYE. . .

Hardly able to contain his coffee-created jitters, Sam sat at his desk. His left knee was bouncing uncontrollably and he was blinking like a kitten with hay fever. It was always tricky for Sam to be quiet, but now it was triply doubly hard.

"Draw an animal found in England," Mrs Mann said. "And no chatting or talking or making any noise while you are drawing – or else."

Sam began to sketch a squirrel and Mrs

Mann patrolled the room, her hands thrust deep into her cardigan pockets, her upright hair perfectly upright. He peeped out from under his blond mop and saw Mrs Mann take one hand from her pocket and shake it, like she was weighing something up. He strained to see. His eyelids twitched. Then quick as a quick flash, Mrs Mann's hand darted out. She was throwing something over the children! What was it? Thanks to all that coffee, Sam was just able to scrawl two words on his notebook, before slipping down, down, down into a deep, dark sleep.

The next thing Sam knew, a car alarm was going off – not Sam's version of one, but a real one – on the street outside. With the noise, the children instantly woke up. They looked around in confusion. What had happened? Had they missed something? Half an hour had passed. Their animal drawings were not finished. What?

"Carry on working, children," said Mrs Mann, looking hugely irritated. "Quickly and quietly."

Sam was confused. He had no idea what had happened. He looked at the sketch pad on his desk and on it, he had written two words:

NECK DUST.

What did NECK DUST mean? Did it

mean anything, or nothing, or something, or nothing again? Sam had no idea, but he guessed that those two words held the key to Mrs Mann and her dodgy plans.

Chapter 17

THE MEANING OF NECK DUST

"Maybe NECK DUST means the dust you find down the back of your neck," said Nina, during lunch break. The pair was watching Jock do high-jump practice with Mr Rump – Jock was leaping about like a kangaroo on a trampoline.

"I dunno," said Sam. "I've never had dust down the back of *my* neck. Crisps, yes, but not dust."

The pair finished their sandwiches, Nina

tucking her knitted lunch box back inside her knitted backpack. Then the pair spotted Bob's Your Uncle sitting outside a shed on the edge of the playing field.

Bob's Your Uncle was listening to his favourite radio programme, *Desert Island Whisks*, in which famous people talk about the whisks that have meant something to them over the years.

"Welcome to my new home," said Bob, as the children approached. "I thought it was best if I stopped using my office, since Mrs Mann closed the stairs. Although I did pop up and fix that door, like you wanted, Sam."

Sam said thanks but he looked worried. "We've got a feeling Mrs Mann is sending us to sleep, but we can't prove it. Has she ever mentioned anything about dust?" he asked.

"Not that I know of, and I am the caretaker

after all – dust in the school is my business!" laughed Bob. "She keeps herself to herself in the staff room. Doesn't talk to anyone. Sits in the corner reading her science and chemistry magazines. And how about this? She never drinks tea! Ever! Extraordinary!"

The children glanced at each other. This was not particularly helpful. They still had no idea what NECK DUST meant.

"Speaking of tea. . ." said Bob.

"No, thanks," said the children.

"Oh, go on," said Bob's Your Uncle. "I've got biscuits. Now, where did I put them?"

Bob rummaged inside his shed for a bit – it was packed with tools and string and rusty tin cans full of screws – and then he disappeared underneath a low shelf, still searching.

"It's no good," Bob said finally, emerging from under the table. "Can't find them. First that storeroom key, now my biscuits. I'd lose my eyebrows if they weren't fixed to my face!"

Sam glanced at Bob's eyebrows and then stared. He couldn't help it! The brows drew him in. They seemed to be moving, like hairy caterpillars doing the conga, and as they moved fluff and dust from under the shelf tumbled from their woolly depths. Fluff and dust. Fluff and . . . DUST!

"I've got it!" Sam yelled.

Bob rubbed his bushy brows and more dust fell out. Sam sneezed. Everyone jumped – man, that sneeze was loud – and then Sam explained.

"I remember now!" Sam said. "Just before I fell asleep, Mrs Mann took some kind of dust out of her pockets, which she threw over us. It lands on our necks when we're bent over our work. That's what puts us to sleep!"

"Neck dust!" said Nina. "Maybe that was what she was making at her last school. The experiment Mr Clod told us about."

"And maybe she used it on Bob, too, so she could steal the key to the storeroom upstairs and use it to hide Mr Clod!" said Sam.

Bob's eyebrows bobbed up and down, like they were floating on the ocean, as he tried to understand what the children were saying.

"Of course!" roared Sam, puzzling even more of the mystery out. "I bet she has used it to keep Mr Clod asleep too, so he didn't make any noise!"

Everyone looked shocked.

"She has tried it on Mr Clod and on us," Sam continued, "and I bet she has plans

to use it right across the town, sending all the children to sleep."

"What do we do?" asked Nina.

"We take Mrs Mann down!" said Sam. "Take her down to Chinatown!"

"Where?" asked Nina.

"Never mind. Tackle her, with my voice," said Sam.

"But you might get hurt, Sam," said Nina. "Shouldn't we just tell Mrs Brisket? Or wait for Mr Clod to come back?"

"She won't believe us!" boomed Sam, feeling fired up. "And who knows when Mr Clod will come back. He wasn't well. Besides," he continued, "this is my fight. I want to show

Mrs Mann that she can't shut us children up. She doesn't get to send us to sleep; not me, not you, not baby Nigel, not anyone. Trust me, Nina, I can do this. Let's find Jock. I have a plan – a plan that will tempt her to act again and then . . . gotcha!"

Chapter 18

HMMMMMMM!

Sam and Nina left Bob's Your Uncle by his shed and ran off to meet Jock. Sam told him his plan, and then, as the bell rang, the three friends went back into the classroom.

When the afternoon was almost over, with just fifteen minutes to go before home time, Sam winked at Jock and Nina and then . . . he started to hum.

Mrs Mann looked up suddenly, like a guard

dog that has sniffed an intruder. Only the intruder was . . . noise!

"Who is humming?" she snapped. "No humming. I forbid it!"

The humming grew louder as Nina and then Jock joined in.

"Quiet!" Mrs Mann barked. "There will be silence, or violence. There is no in-between!"

The three children hummed louder still. The rest of the class looked excited, but nervous too (except Jeremy Fortesque Winterflunkett, who just looked annoyed). It sounded like a swarm of wasps doing laps of the classroom on mopeds.

Mrs Mann jumped up from her desk, her

tiny eyes blazing with fury, her hair . . . well, her hair didn't do anything. It was rigid, as usual.

"I am hearing things, and I want to be hearing *no* things!" she said.

The humming continued.

"Noise annoys, remember?" she snapped. "If you are not silent in three seconds, I will put all your names on the noise polluters list! The loudness must end!"

But the loudness did not end. It continued. Mrs Mann quickly rummaged in her beehive and pulled out a small hammer which she banged on the desk.

"Silence!" she barked.

Still the humming droned on.

"Sam Lowe!" shouted Mrs Mann. "I can tell you are humming. You're much louder than everyone else. You will all stop now or Sam will have to bath Hugo, *and* polish his eyes, *every day for a month*!"

Sam, Nina and Jock fell silent immediately. That was just too icky a task to inflict on anyone and besides, Stage One of the plan was complete. Mrs Mann tucked the hammer back into her hair and sat, seething, for the last few minutes of the day. When the bell went and Sam left the classroom, he could feel her eyes on his back (not literally, of course –

her eyes were still in her head, just below her eyebrows, where you'd expect them to be).

"I have a feeling Monday is the day!" Sam said to Nina. "We extra, extra annoyed Mrs Mann just now. She won't want a repeat of that humming again," said Sam. "No, she will want . . . *revenge*!"

Chapter 19

COUNTDOWN TO A SHOWDOWN

As preparation for Stage Two of his plan, Sam spent the weekend practising his shock wave and all his super-loud voices. He even managed to see Bryce Canyon. The speech therapist didn't usually work at the weekends, but Sam called him and asked for a special appointment. So on Saturday afternoon, in Bryce's office, Sam ran through his voices, trying them at different volumes, waiting to see what Bryce would say.

"Good," Bryce said. "You sound strong and,

more importantly, in control, Sam. I'm proud of you."

Sam blushed and looked down. And then he remembered the comic Bryce had given him and went to hand it back.

"It's yours," said Bryce, smiling warmly. "You have more in common with the hero in those pages than you even realize. Good job. Now get out of here!" And he winked at Sam.

Nina, meanwhile, spent the weekend knitting. On the way into school on Monday, she handed Sam a woolly hat with the initials SL on it.

"I made this for you," said Nina. "It looks

like a regular bobble hat, but I've made some modifications, as discussed."

Sam examined the hat and smiled.

"It's fantastic," he said.

Nina nodded seriously. "Cheeses come and go, but a good hat sticks like toffee," she said, making no sense. Or maybe just a bit of sense. Sam wasn't sure.

"Everyone will think the initials on it stand for Sam Lowe," Nina went on. "But we know they are your secret identity. We know they stand for. . ."

"SUPER LOUD!" roared Sam, pulling the hat on to his head and giving the thumbs up to a van full of builders who, startled by Sam's mega shout, had spilled tea down their overalls.

Jock had rounded up all their classmates in the playground by the time Sam and Nina arrived. Everyone listened carefully to what Sam had to say.

"Children, classmates, friends," said Sam

in his big, clear voice. "There is a super villain among us!"

The children looked nervously at one another. Then Sam explained how he suspected Mrs Mann was putting them to sleep. With weird dust! And how the humming on Friday was a way to make her angry, so that she was bound to put them to sleep today, right now!

Most of the children nodded, wide eyed, as they began to understand, but not everyone was sure about Sam's ideas.

"You don't know what you're jolly well talking about," huffed Jeremy Fortesque Winterflunkett. "Or shouting about, I should say."

A few children giggled.

"Do you have a better explanation for what's happening?" Sam asked, feeling suddenly brave, his golden hair glowing in the sunlight like a lion's mane. "We can't be falling asleep just because Mrs Mann is rubbish and boring. No teacher could be boring enough to send every one of us to sleep for a whole day."

Jeremy was about to say something, but Sam carried on.

"You have to believe me. We think Mrs Mann has some kind of magic powder that she uses to send us to sleep," said Sam. "I've seen how dangerous it can be. You don't remember, but when you're sleepy, you leave school and get into terrible danger."

"We also believe she has plans to spread the sleep to other schools in the area," added Nina. "Silencing all children! Stopping our fun! Spoiling our lives! We cannot let this happen."

Then Jock broke yet more shocking news: "Mrs Mann has been keeping Mr Clod prisoner upstairs, too," he said, a fact which drew gasps from the children. "But luckily, Sam here can tackle her."

"Since when was Sam Lowe such a hero?" Jeremy grumbled.

"Since he saved us all from having awful accidents when we were sleepy!" said Jock.

"Since he blasted a door down with his voice and rescued Mr Clod from the storeroom! Since he decided he would tackle a teacher who is out of control and a danger to all children in Topside! *That's* when."

It was quite a speech from Jock, who was, after all, something of a school legend. Now, any children who had their doubts, binned their doubts, and stared at Sam with a look of wonder and, yes, respect in their eyes (and no doubts at all). Agatha Ackerbilk actually clapped. Sam felt proud; more proud than a gardener who's just won gold for his prize marrow at the village show.

"But what can we do?" asked Agatha. "How

can we help you, Sam?"

"Just protect yourselves," said Sam, "and trust me. Nina?"

Nina stepped forward and handed each of her classmates a woolly scarf that she had knitted over the weekend.

"Wear them in class," Sam said to his friends. "They may offer some protection from the dust. Good luck."

And then Sam hugged Nina and shook Jock's hand.

"Show time!" he said, and the three friends went inside.

Chapter 20

MANN VS SAM

In the classroom, Mrs Mann was standing at the front, looking fierce in her grey cardigan. She glared at the children and their unusual knitwear as they filed in, but said nothing.

"There will be no repeat of the humming stupidity of Friday," Mrs Mann said. "Today, we shall have silence. Or else."

The children sat down quietly. Sam pulled his hat more firmly on to his head and peeped at his teacher. He pretended to work on his picture, but kept glancing up at Mrs Mann as she walked between the desks. Sam felt his heart racing as Mrs Mann reached into her pocket . . . and then pulled out a hankie and blew her nose. Phewww! Sam breathed out heavily.

More minutes of quiet drawing passed. Maybe Mrs Mann would not strike today? Perhaps Sam had got it all wrong? He peeped at his teacher again. That's when he saw Mrs Mann reach her hand into her pocket – and it happened! Her hand darted out, scattering a fine spray of dust that spread around the classroom.

The dust found its way under and through

the scarves, and most of the children crumpled on to their desks – but not everybody. Jeremy Fortesque Winterflunkett tried to bolt, but his scarf tumbled off as he ran and that was Mrs Mann's chance. Soon Jeremy was sound asleep on the grey carpet.

Next, Aaron Abacus tried a commando crawl under the desks. He was almost at the exit when Mrs Mann grabbed him by his scarf and pulled him upright. The she flicked a pinch of dust at the boy, whose legs immediately went to jelly and sent him tumbling to the floor, fast asleep.

Now Mrs Mann turned towards Sam, who was standing at the back of the class. Jock and Nina spied their chance. They tiptoed silently behind a bookcase, where they hid as their teacher called out to Sam.

"Lowe!" she said, walking slowly towards him. "Time for sleep, I think! A nice, quiet sleep, so I can have a nice, quiet day."

Sam stared back, almost too scared to move. And then he heard a voice – a deep, soft, wise voice. It was Bryce Canyon again, the super-cool speech therapist, speaking inside Sam's brain.

Use the hat, Sam, Bryce said. *Use the hat on your head.*

Of course! He'd nearly forgotten.

Sam swiftly unrolled the hat's thick rim, and in an instant his innocent bobble hat was transformed into a woolly mask fit for a super hero. Oh, Nina, well done! It covered Sam's face and neck, with just three little slits for his eyes and mouth. It gave Sam power and confidence and. . .

WHAM!

He boomed out his earth-shaking shock wave. The blast picked up some pencils and they flew at Mrs Mann like tiny arrows. Mrs Mann whipped her cardigan up like a woolly bullfighter's cape, and the pencils ricocheted off in all directions.

No matter, thought Sam. *There's more where that came from.*

BOOM!

Sam let go another shock wave, blasting books at Mrs Mann, but these just bounced off her cardigan, too, as if they were autumn leaves blown from a tree. The naughty teacher stood firm.

OK, thought Sam, *she seems to be stronger than I had guessed, but don't panic.*

Another **BOOM** and Sam picked up Hugo, flinging the stuffed cat towards Mrs Mann's face. But she just raised a fist and punched her former pet clean away. *BOOF!* Nasty!

"I do not tolerate noise in my classroom, Sam Lowe," Mrs Mann said, walking towards him.

"Well, bad luck," said Sam, "because I'm not Sam Lowe, see? I am Super Loud!"

With this, Sam unleashed his full, super-loud voice. A volcano of volume exploded in the classroom. Mrs Mann clamped her hands over her ears and shrunk from the sound. She tottered backwards, her tiny eyes wide with shock. Now Sam switched back to the shock wave and blasted out a powerful ripple, which pinned Mrs Mann against the whiteboard and sent scissors flying towards her, like darts towards a dartboard.

THUD-THUD-THUD-THUD-THUD! The scissors hit the whiteboard, pinning Mrs Mann in place by her cardigan. She was stuck. Skewered in place. Sam had done it. His body sagged with relief. His throat felt dry and tight. But no matter. It was over.

ZZZz
Zzzzz

Chapter 21

ER, NOT *QUITE* OVER, ACTUALLY

That's right. Sam thought his epic battle with his villainous teacher was over, and turned away to catch his breath, but he was wrong.

"Look out!" yelled Nina, sticking her head out from behind the bookcase.

Like King Kong breaking loose from his chains, the mighty Mann was ripping her cardigan free of its scissory bonds. She marched towards Sam again. She reached into her pockets, grabbed a handful of dust and threw it. Sam ducked. A little dust hit his head but his hat-mask protected him.

Mrs Mann was furious now, but Sam stood firm. He opened his mouth to roar at her again, took in a deep breath, puffed out his chest for one final blast and. . .

No sound came out! Sam shook his head. What? He tried again and again, but each time – nothing!

Where there should have been

a super-loud voice, there was just a miserable croak. Disaster! Calamity! Very bad indeed! In all the blasting and booming, the impossible and very last thing Sam could want to happen, had happened.

Sam had lost his voice!!

When Mrs Mann realized what had happened she stood still and laughed. It was the first time Sam had heard her laugh. Well, it was more of a cackle, really. Not a pretty sound.

"Lost your voice, have you?" she said. "Pity!"

Mrs Mann cackled some more. Wow, she was really enjoying this. As she wiped a tear of mirth from her tiny, dark eyes, Sam caught sight of Nina crawling beneath desks, trying to get close to him.

"I knew from the second I saw you, Sam, that we were not going to get on," Mrs Mann said. "The kind of noise you produce is a curse. You need to learn that noise is bad and pointless, just as I did. . ."

Sam glanced at Nina, who was crawling closer. Mrs Mann had not seen her. She was too busy with her monologue.

"I was on holiday in Devon years ago when I learned to hate noise. I was looking forward to a quiet break, away from lessons and squawking children, and planned to enjoy some of the local toffee. . .'

Nina was really close now.

"But my holiday cottage was next to a *nursery*!" Mrs Mann spat out the word "nursery" like it tasted of mouldy muffins.

"All day, the tiny children yelled and laughed. I couldn't think. I couldn't relax. So I moved to a different hotel, but it was next to a *playground*!"

Again, you'd think the word "playground" tasted of earwax, the way Mrs Mann said it.

"Oh, how the children shrieked and wailed," Mrs Mann continued. "I tried to ignore the noise and enjoy my toffee, but my hands became fists and crushed the sticky sweeties. The noise made me furious and I ran my hands through my hair, over and over, tearing at it because of the racket. The result? I hated noise from that day on, and my hair became stuck vertically upwards as you see it now. A giant, hairy exclamation mark!"

For a second, Mrs Mann gazed out of the window, lost in her bitter memories. And just at that moment. . .

"Sam, catch!" shouted Nina.

Nina threw a water bottle towards Sam. He jumped for it, but was too slow. Mrs Mann's quick hands darted out and grabbed the bottle.

"NO. YOU. DON'T!" she hissed, pinging

her attention back on Sam. "I plan to silence all the children in this town, school by school, and you will not stop me. That Clod couldn't stop me. He helped me, in fact. My dust was too strong for Hugo, but I practised on Mr Clod until I made it just right. And with him

locked in the storeroom, I was free to try it on all of you. Now I know my dust works; I know its power. Now nobody can stand in my way!"

Then she turned Sam's water bottle upside down and poured the water out. Nina gasped as it cascaded down. So did Sam – but in a cool Super Loud way. Oh yes! He bossed it! Instead of booming his voice out, Sam breathed it in, scooping up the water and sucking it straight into his mouth!

GULP!

"Now *that's* better!" said Sam, and he unleashed his final weapon.

"WHEEEE-WHEEEE-WHEEEE," Sam went. Jeepers, that car alarm was loud! So loud and ear-splitting that all the other children woke up – *DING!* – just like that.

So loud that Mrs Mann covered her ears and cringed.

"No, Sam!" she said. "It's too much! Stop the alarm! I command you! OR!! ELSE!!!"

Fat chance. Sam didn't stop and wouldn't stop. He kept on car-alarming, marching on Mrs Mann with his mighty sound.

Still holding her ears, Mrs Mann stumbled backwards up the classroom. All the children watched, amazed. Then she dropped to her knees and crawled under her desk. There was a tinkling sound, and Bob's key to the upstairs storeroom where Mr Clod had been trapped dropped from her hair on to the carpet.

"Ha! So she did steal that key!" said Nina.

Sam couldn't reply. He didn't dare stop the car-alarm sound until Mrs Brisket, with

Miss Hash scurrying along behind, marched into the classroom. And what a strange sight greeted them – a gaggle of excited children, a boy in a red woolly mask making a noise like a car alarm, and a quivering teacher, crouched beneath her desk.

Chapter 22

THE TRUTH IS OUT THERE

"What on *earth* is going on?" asked Mrs Brisket, waving her ear trumpet at the children.

Sam stopped *WHEEEE*ing, pulled off his hat-mask and explained. "Mrs Mann has been putting us to sleep," he said, panting a little. "She uses some special dust that she keeps in her pockets and scatters it on us so we fall asleep all day."

"It's true," said Nina. Mrs Brisket put the

trumpet into her ear and nodded at Nina to go on. "She hates noise, so she puts us to sleep. But then it's really hard to wake up, which is why there was that funny sleepwalking problem after school."

"She also plans to silence all the schools in Topside," added Jock, pulling the map out from Mrs Mann's desk drawer and showing it to the head teacher. "She has to be stopped or the town's children will never have fun again."

Mrs Brisket, speechless, looked towards Mrs Mann for an explanation. Mrs Mann had crawled out from under her desk and was patting her tower of hair.

"I can assure you that everything these

children say is entirely untrue," said Mrs Mann, acting as if what had just happened hadn't just happened. "Sam was being a little noisy this morning, but I have dealt with it now."

"But you were under your desk!" Mrs Brisket spluttered.

"I dropped a biscuit," said Mrs Mann. "A custard cream."

Mrs Brisket didn't know what to say – about the custard cream or anything else. Frowning, she thanked Mrs Mann and turned to leave the classroom, when Nina stopped her.

"Look, Mrs Brisket!" said Nina, pointing at a film of dust on the desk. Nina scraped it off and tipped it into Mrs Brisket's hand. "This is the magic dust."

Mrs Brisket looked at it for a while, as if she were about to take the children seriously, but then she tutted.

"I need to have a word with Caretaker Bob," she said. "He has obviously not been cleaning thoroughly enough."

And then, using her ear trumpet as a blowpipe, she blew the dust off her hands.

Nina looked horrified, the children looked shocked and Mrs Mann's eyes sparkled with delight, but Sam had a brilliant idea. Forming an O with his mouth, he created one final shock wave. As the dust floated towards the floor, the blast picked it up and blew it – straight into Mrs Mann's face!

With one almighty sneeze, the terrible noise-hating teacher collapsed on the floor. She was fast asleep.

The children cheered and Sam let out a huge, mighty whoop of joy that could be heard half a mile away!

"My goodness," said Mrs Brisket, once the celebrations had died down. "I think I owe you an apology." Then she pointed at the unconscious teacher. "Now then, Sam," she said. "How do we wake her up?"

Chapter 23

SHE'S A BAD MANN

You will be pleased to hear that Mrs Mann never taught at Topside Junior School again. Sam woke her up with a quick car-alarm blast, but not before the police came to arrest the troublesome teacher.

Mrs Mann was taken to the police station and soon a sinister story of lies, more lies and a few extra lies on top emerged about the wicked teacher's background, all of which Bob told the children over a cup of tea in his room.

"Turns out Mrs Mann had a whole chemistry lab in her house," said Bob. "She'd been developing this crazy dust for years. There were jars of it everywhere. She also made a dust for waking people up, but she hadn't really tried it out," Bob's Your Uncle continued. "That's why you lot were so groggy that day after school."

"We were right about the other schools, too," asked Sam. "She wanted to silence all the children in Topside, didn't she?"

"Quite right!" said Bob, his eyebrows beaming above his smiling face. "Mrs Mann wanted to become head of Topside Junior School and from there, take on the rest of the town and its noisy children. But she hadn't reckoned on Sam and his super-loud voice, had she?"

Sam grinned. Success tasted sweet, like a giant fruit gum dipped in syrup. After all, Mrs Mann, the cardigan-wearing, noise-naysayer, was defeated by just the kind of noisy boy she was trying to silence. Perfect! And, as Nina pointed out, "Victory is a sausage best served sizzling."

Mrs Mann was fined loads of money for her ill-doings, and went to live on a remote island somewhere remote. Bob, meanwhile, was asked to give her classroom a thorough clean to remove every last trace of the dangerous dust.

If you had watched Bob go about this serious cleaning job, you would have seen him enter the room holding two handheld vacuum cleaners like guns in holsters. For Bob's dreams of being a cowboy had never completely left him. He lifted them up, glanced around the room, muttered, "If you're looking for trouble, dust, you've come to the right place," and clicked them on.

VROOOM!

Then he vacuumed the room.

Chapter 24

HIP HIP HOORAY!

To thank Sam for his shouting showdown, he was given Topside Junior School's highest award – the Golden Topside Trophy. Sam's mum came to school to see Sam receive it. Sam looked proud as a parsnip, standing on stage while Mrs Brisket made a speech.

"You truly are a hero, Sam," said Mrs Brisket. "We have sometimes encouraged you to be quiet, but now we recognize that your loud voice is your greatest strength. Well done! You saved us all!"

Then Mrs Brisket blew a little blast on her ear trumpet – *TOOT TOOT!* – which was a nice touch, and all the children cheered and laughed.

There was a special guest in the audience too – Mr Clod.

"I'm so sorry, Sam," he said. "I meant to come back to school, to explain everything to Mrs Brisket and help you sort out Mrs Mann, but I got home, ate a big bowl of pasta and then just fell asleep again. I only woke up when Mrs Brisket came to my house to tell me what had happened. I guess that sleeping drug was still sloshing about in my system, making me dead to the world!"

"No problem, sir," said Sam.

"No, indeed. You sent Mrs Mann packing with your amazing voice," said Mr Clod. "In fact, your voice reminds me of that time I was working as a DJ on an airfield in Morocco. Very noisy! I must tell you about that someday."

Sam's classmates huddled around him, too, patting him on the back. Mr Rump said, "Well done, son," and even Jeremy Fortesque Winterflunkett admitted Sam had done a "first-class job".

Nina presented Sam with a special medal

she had knitted and Jock slapped his new friend hard on the back.

"Excellent!" he said. "It's just all so excellent! And you are one excellent guy!"

And then Bob's Your Uncle raised a finger in the air, caught everyone's attention and said:

"I know just the thing to help us celebrate. Tea!"

Chapter 25

THE BRYCE IS RIGHT

There was one person Sam was desperate to share his news with – Bryce Canyon. So, a few days later, Sam called at Bryce's office, clutching the Golden Trophy in one hand. There was nobody at the reception desk and when Sam knocked on Bryce's door, a woman answered.

"He moved out," said the woman. "I use this office now. I make greetings cards."

She invited Sam to take a look. There were

cards everywhere. Some were cute. (Sam noticed a card with two kittens cuddling a chick on it – adorable!) Other cards simply carried messages.

Sam picked one up. BE YOURSELF, it said.

"Take it, if you like," said the woman.

"Thank you," said Sam, and left.

Be yourself, thought Sam as he walked home. It felt like the kind of advice Bryce might give him. Sam didn't understand why Bryce had left so suddenly, but the card seemed like a final message from him.

"All right!" thought Sam. "I *will* be myself."

He pulled his SL hat on over his messy hair

and then, grinning and running and swinging his backpack around, Sam let one mighty, magnificent roar:

"I AM SUPER LOUD!"

A QUICK SHOUT-OUT FOR OTHER BOOKS BY JO SIMMONS!

PIP STREET
Jo Simmons
The Great Kitty Kidnap
"Utterly charming and delightful"
Mel Giedroyc

PIP STREET
Jo Simmons
The Pesky Pig Panic
"Utterly charming and delightful"
Mel Giedroyc

PIP STREET
Jo Simmons
The Crazy Crumpet Kerfuffle
"Utterly charming and delightful"
Mel Giedroyc

PIP STREET
Jo Simmons
The Big Brother Bother
"Utterly charming and delightful"
Mel Giedroyc

SL